Hiya! My name Thudd. Best robot friend of Drewd. Thudd know lots of stuff. Why ocean is salty. How octopus change color. Why continents always moving.

Drewd like to invent stuff. Thudd help! Now Drewd help Uncle Al make new underwater invention. Oop! Accident happen! Adventure happen! Want to come along? Look for giant squid? Turn page, please!

Get lost with
Andrew, Judy, and Thudd
in all their exciting adventures!

ANDREW LOST

8

IN THE DEEP

BY J. C. GREENBURG

ILLUSTRATED
BY JAN GERARDI

A STEPPING STONE BOOK™

Random House New York

To Dan and Zack and Dad
and the real Andrew, with love.
And to Jim Thomas, Mallory Loehr,
and all my Random House friends,
with an ocean of thanks.
—J.C.G.

www.randomhouse.com/kids
www.AndrewLost.com

Library of Congress Cataloging-in-Publication Data
Greenburg, J. C. (Judith C.)
In the deep / by J. C. Greenburg ; illustrated by Jan Gerardi. — 1st ed.
    p.   cm. — (Andrew Lost ; 8)   "A stepping stone book."
SUMMARY: Still trying to save the giant squid from Soggy Bob, ten-year-old Andrew, his cousin Judy, and Thudd the robot nearly meet disaster at the Challenger Deep, the deepest place in the ocean.
ISBN 0-375-82526-6 (trade) — ISBN 0-375-92526-0 (lib. bdg.)
[1. Marine animals—Fiction. 2. Giant squids—Fiction.
3. Squids—Fiction. 4. Cousins—Fiction.] I. Gerardi, Jan, ill.
II. Title. III. Series: Greenburg, J. C. (Judith C.). Andrew Lost ; v 8.
PZ7.G82785 Ine 2004   [Fic]—dc22   2003018152

Printed in the United States of America
First Edition 10 9 8 7 6 5 4 3 2 1

THUDD

CONTENTS

ANDREW'S WORLD

Andrew Dubble

Andrew is ten years old, but he's been inventing things since he was four. Andrew's inventions usually get him into trouble, like the time he shrunk himself, his cousin Judy, and his little silver robot Thudd smaller than a bee's knees with the Atom Sucker.

But today Andrew is in the biggest trouble he's ever been in. He fooled around with his Uncle Al's underwater vehicle, the Water Bug. Now Andrew, Judy, and Thudd are headed for the deepest, most dangerous place on earth!

Judy Dubble

Judy is Andrew's thirteen-year-old cousin. She's been on four safaris to Africa. But today she's going to a place where only two other humans have been before. . . .

Thudd

The Handy Ultra-Digital Detective. Thudd is

a super-smart robot and Andrew's best friend. When Andrew and Judy were lost on the reef, Thudd saved them from tiny—and deadly—blue-ringed octopuses. Can Thudd help Andrew and Judy save the giant squids?

Uncle Al

Andrew and Judy's uncle is a top-secret scientist. He invented Thudd and the Water Bug. Now he's finishing up a new underwater vehicle called the See Horse so that he can rescue Andrew, Judy, and Thudd!

The Water Bug

It used to be an old Volkswagen Beetle until Uncle Al turned it into a submarine. Now it has a glass floor, a sharky fin on its roof, and a bathroom in the back. It's headed for a place where the water will press against it like tons of elephants. Is it strong enough not to be crushed?

Soggy Bob Sloggins

This bad guy of the sea is building Animal Universe, the biggest theme park in the world. But Soggy Bob doesn't care about the animals. He hung a sign above the aquarium in Squid World. It says SOGGY BOB'S GIANT SQUIDWICHES—COMING SOON! Will Andrew, Judy, and Thudd find the giant squid in time to stop Soggy Bob from turning it into giant snacks? Will *anyone* find the giant squid? After all, no human has ever seen a giant squid alive. . . .

1 NIGHT LIGHTS

Ten-year-old Andrew Dubble was zooming through the ocean in his uncle's underwater vehicle, the Water Bug.

All through the dark water, sparks of blue light exploded like mini-fireworks.

The headlights of the Water Bug fell on huge dish-y shapes swooping closer and closer.

Those couldn't *be flying saucers,* Andrew thought. *We're underwater, so they'd have to be* swimming *saucers!*

Next to Andrew sat his thirteen-year-old cousin Judy. This morning, Andrew and Judy had been getting ready to fly home from their vacation in Hawai'i. But Andrew made a little mistake. Now they were on their way to save the giant squids!

The flying-saucer shapes were right in front of the Water Bug's headlights. The shapes had giant mouths. They were wide open!

"Cheese Louise!" said Judy. "What *are* those things? Their mouths are big enough to swallow us!"

meep . . . "Manta ray!" came a squeaky voice from the front pocket of Andrew's underwater suit. It was Thudd, Andrew's little silver robot and best friend.

meep . . . "Manta ray not eat people. Just eat tiny stuff. Manta mouth like big net."

Judy frowned. "That's what you said *right before we got swallowed by a blue whale!*"

The manta rays tumbled around the Water Bug, gobbling up the mini-fireworks.

"Jeepers creepers!" said Andrew. "They're eating those little lights!"

meep . . . "Ocean animals with light inside," said Thudd. "Called bioluminescence."

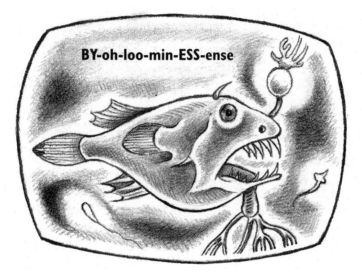

BY-oh-loo-min-ESS-ense

"Oh yeah!" said Andrew. "Living light! Like we saw in the underwater cave."

"Yoop!" squeaked Thudd. "Animals use living light to find mate. Find prey. Sometimes scare predator. Like big camera flash in face! Ocean got lotsa living light. Look!"

Thudd pointed outside. The dark ocean twinkled with a zillion tiny lights.

Judy leaned over and tapped the compass in the middle of the Water Bug's steering wheel.

"Hey, Bug-Brain," she said to Andrew. "Why don't you watch where we're going?"

The words GIANT SQUID were lit up in green letters at the top of the compass. But the compass arrow was pointing away from the words.

"Oops!" said Andrew. He turned the steering wheel and the arrow zinged toward the green words.

glurp . . . "Thank you," came the voice of the Water Bug. "We are now back on the trail of the giant squid."

Suddenly the manta rays flapped away like a flock of giant flying pancakes. Coming toward them was a fish twice as long as the Water Bug!

The fish swam closer. Sticking out of its nose was a long, flat paddle with big teeth all along the edge.

"Wowzers schnauzers!" said Andrew. "It looks like a swimming chain saw!"

meep . . . "Sawfish!" said Thudd.

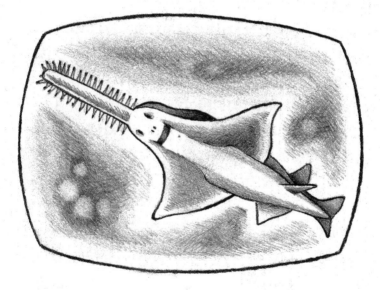

"It looks like something Soggy Bob invented to chop up the Water Bug," said Judy.

Soggy Bob Sloggins was searching for the giant squids, too. But he didn't want to save them. He wanted to turn them into squidwiches for his Animal Universe theme park!

Andrew, Judy, and Thudd were trying to stop him.

meep . . . "Sawfish not use saw to hurt people," said Thudd. "Saw feel electricity that come from all living things. Use saw to find little crabs and fish in mud and dig them up."

"Neato mosquito," said Andrew. "The sawfish has its own tool kit!"

Suddenly from behind the sawfish came a flashing light. It wasn't the random glimmer of sea creatures. There was a pattern: three short flashes, three long ones, then three short ones again.

"It's a signal in Morse code!" said Judy. "Mom and Dad taught me Morse code before they took me on my first African safari."

"What does it mean?" asked Andrew.

"Three short flashes mean 'S,'" said Judy. "The long ones mean 'O.' . . . So the message says 'SOS.' That's the code word for 'Help'!"

The sawfish began to circle the Water Bug.

"Look!" said Andrew. "There's a rope around the sawfish's tail!"

At the end of the rope was a huge white egg with big metal claws. The bright flashes were coming from a window at the front of the egg!

2 SINKING!

"It's the Egg-Mobile!" said Andrew.

Through the egg's window, Andrew and Judy saw a big blue parrot. It was flapping its wings frantically.

"That's Burpp inside!" said Judy.

"Burpp" was short for **B**ob's **U**ltra-**R**obot **P**arrot **P**artner. Burpp belonged to Soggy Bob Sloggins.

"Burpp looks scared," said Judy.

"Holy moly," said Andrew. "The Egg-Mobile has big cracks in it. I think we have to rescue Burpp!"

"But what if this is a trick?" said Judy.

"What if we rescue Burpp and he tries to take over the Water Bug?"

Andrew thought for a moment. "We'll tie him up before we let him in," he said.

Andrew pressed a black button on the dashboard and spoke into a microphone. "Cut the rope," he said. "Get Burpp out of the Egg-Mobile and use the rope to tie him up. Then bring Burpp into the Water Bug."

glurp . . . "A bad idea," said the Water Bug. "But if you insist . . ."

The hood of the Water Bug popped open. The long gray tentacles of the Octo-Tool twirled out from under the hood. One of the tentacles carried scissors. Lightning fast, it cut the rope that tied the Egg-Mobile to the saw-fish's tail. The sawfish sped away.

The other tentacles yanked at the window of the Egg-Mobile. The window was also the Egg-Mobile's door. But the tentacles couldn't open it.

Three of the tentacles ducked back under the hood. When they came out again, they were carrying hammers. They began to bang away at the white shell. Inside the Egg-Mobile, Burpp pecked the walls with his beak.

KRAAACK!

The giant egg split in two! Burpp tumbled out. The Octo-Tool tentacles grabbed Burpp,

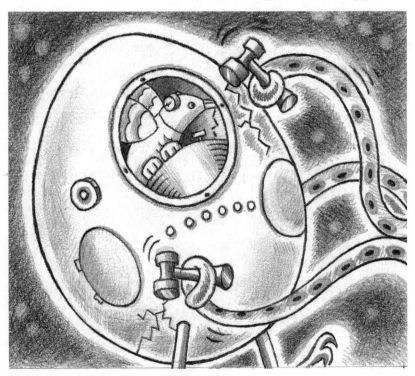

tied up his feet, and towed him under the hood of the Water Bug.

A few seconds later, two big parrot feet poked through the rubber flap under the Water Bug's steering wheel. Andrew yanked one foot and Judy tugged the other.

Awk! "Thank you! Thank you! Thank you!" Burpp squawked from under the hood.

"Wait a minute," said Judy. She stopped tugging Burpp's foot and made Andrew stop, too.

"Can we really trust you?" she asked.

Awk! "Promise!" said Burpp. "On my bird of honor!"

"You'd better be telling the truth," said Judy. She grabbed a scaly leg and pulled. "Moof!" she groaned. "I think he's stuck."

"Oofers!" said Andrew. "This isn't easy!"

Awk! "This not easy for Burpp, either!" squawked Burpp. "Burpp is getting squashed down to parakeet size!"

"One, two, three . . . PULL!" said Judy.

Klink, klink, klink . . .

With a tinkle of metal feathers, Burpp burst through the flap.

Burpp's wing smacked Judy in the nose and poked Thudd out of Andrew's pocket.

"You'll have to get in the back," said Judy, shoving Burpp's tail feathers over the front seats.

Instead of having a backseat like other cars, the Water Bug had a tiny bathroom and a kitchen.

Burpp landed between the bathroom door and the kitchen sink.

Awk! "Burpp is grateful to you, little Dubbles!" said Burpp. "Soggy Bob left the Egg-Mobile stuck on the coral reef. Then Burpp saw the sawfish. Burpp used the Egg-Mobile claws to rope him! The sawfish pulled the Egg-Mobile off the reef.

"But the Egg-Mobile hit a rock. Everything broke! No power! No steering! The claws wouldn't let go of the rope! Burpp could have been stuck to the tail of that sawfish forever!"

Andrew looked Burpp in the eye. "You know we've got to find the giant squids before Soggy Bob does," he said. "We can't let Soggy Bob turn them into giant squid-wiches."

Awk! "Burpp will help you!" said Burpp. "Soggy Bob is loony as a gooney bird and only getting worse!"

"Okay," said Andrew. "Let's go! Judy, untie Burpp's feet."

Andrew pressed the gas pedal. But instead of speeding ahead, the Water Bug bounced up and down in the water like a pogo stick.

Kerchunk . . . kerchunk . . . kerchunk . . .

"Uh-oh," said Andrew. The Water Bug began to zigzag down.

Blurghhhh . . .

It sputtered and sank. The buttons and dials on the dashboard blinked. The head-lights flickered.

"Cheese Louise!" said Judy. "We're losing power and sinking fast!"

SHRINKING!

"What's going on, Water Bug?" Andrew asked. "Are you out of fuel or something?"

glurp . . . "Checking, checking, checking," said the Water Bug. "Do not know."

Judy turned to Burpp and pushed her face close to his beak.

"Did you do something to the Water Bug?" she asked.

Awk! "Burpp didn't do *anything*!" said Burpp, chewing on a broken claw. "*Please* don't blame Burpp!"

"Thudd," said Andrew, "call Uncle Al."

meep . . . "Okey-dokey," said Thudd.

Uncle Al was Andrew and Judy's uncle and a top-secret scientist. He invented Thudd and the Water Bug.

Thudd pressed the big purple button in the middle of his chest.

The purple button blinked three times.

The Water Bug kept drifting down. Outside, animals that looked like strings of Christmas lights fluttered through the darkness.

"Look!" said Andrew. He pointed to a red jellyfish as big as a washing machine.

A long, skinny fish zipped by. Lights glowed along its side like the windows of a spaceship.

A squad of umbrella-shaped squids floated up to the windshield.

"Wowzers!" said Andrew. "These guys are amazing!"

Up and down the arms of the squids ran dots of flashlight-bright colors—blue and yellow, purple and red. Even the squids' eyes sparkled with light.

meep . . . "Squids got living light, too," said Thudd.

Awk! "Maybe the squids are sending a message," said Burpp.

Suddenly the hood of the Water Bug started to flash colors. It flickered sky blue, then leaf green, then pearly pink.

"Jumping gerbils!" said Andrew. "The Protectum coating is going wild!"

glurp . . . "Telling squids we come as friends," said the Water Bug.

Judy's eyes narrowed. "Cut the squid chat," she said. "Let's get the Water Bug fixed! Now!"

"Oh, right!" said Andrew. He pushed buttons and turned dials. But still nothing happened.

They drifted deeper and deeper.

Strange new creatures prowled the night ocean. With their jagged shapes and awful mouths, they could have hatched from bad dreams.

Some had fangs so long they couldn't close their mouths. One looked like a giant mouth attached to a long sock. Some looked like messy piles of seaweed with mouths in the middle.

One wide-open mouth had a light inside. A tiny fish swam up to the light, and the mouth snapped it up!

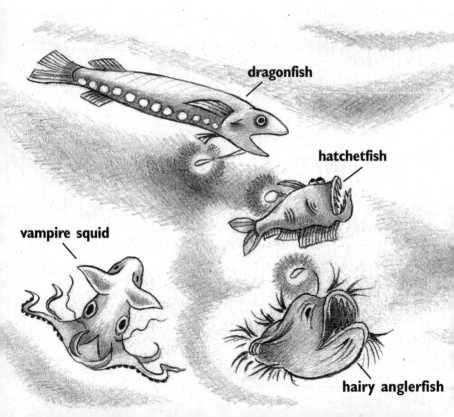

dragonfish

hatchetfish

vampire squid

hairy anglerfish

As the parade of creatures glided and squirmed by, Thudd squeaked out their names: dragonfish, hatchetfish, gulper eel, fangtooth, ghost shark, saber-toothed viperfish!

Suddenly the big purple button in the middle of Thudd's chest began to blink. It popped open and a beam of purple light zoomed out.

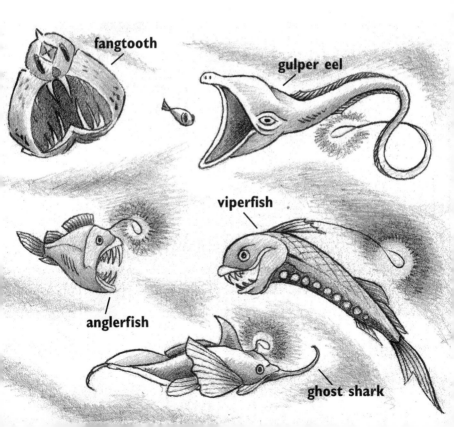

fangtooth

gulper eel

viperfish

anglerfish

ghost shark

A hologram of
Uncle Al appeared
on the dashboard.

"Hi there, guys!"
said Uncle Al.

He was smiling,
but he looked tired.

His shaggy hair was even shaggier than usual.

"Hi, Uncle Al!" said Andrew.

"Hiya, Unkie," said Thudd.

Awk! "Hello, Professor Dubble!" said Burpp.

"We've got a problem!" said Judy.

"I'm not surprised," said Uncle Al. "And
it sounds like you've got Soggy Bob's parrot
with you! I hope he's not the problem."

When Uncle Al visited them by hologram, he could hear them but not see them.

"We had to rescue Burpp," said Andrew.
"He's on our side now."

"The bad news," said Judy, "is that the
Water Bug lost power and is sinking!"

GRAAACK! came a sound from the back of the Water Bug.

Andrew and Judy turned to see what had happened. A lightning-shaped crack ran half-way down the rear window!

"The back window cracked!" yelled Judy.

Uncle Al's bushy eyebrows tilted up to his shaggy hair. "Uh, that's because the Water Bug is shrinking," he said.

4 MELTING!

meep . . . "Water Bug more than mile deep now," said Thudd. "Lotsa water press against Water Bug. Water heavy, heavy, heavy! Like big giraffe sitting on every inch of Water Bug."

"That's dumb," said Judy. "Giraffes are too big to fit on an inch of anything."

Uncle Al interrupted her. "A big giraffe weighs about three thousand pounds," he said. "Three thousand pounds of water are pressing against every inch of the Water Bug. The amount of water that presses against something is called water pressure.

"But don't worry about the window," said Uncle Al. "The water pressure will probably hold it in place."

"Probably?" yelled Judy. "'Probably' is not the word you want to hear when you're more than a mile under the ocean!"

Uncle Al nodded. "I understand," he said. "But don't worry. I've finished the See Horse and am on my way to find you."

The See Horse was a new underwater vehicle that Uncle Al had been working on.

Uncle Al rubbed his chin and frowned. "I just hope you're not anywhere near a certain place."

"What place is that?" asked Judy.

"It's called the Challenger Deep," said Uncle Al. "It's the deepest place in the ocean."

meep . . . "Seven miles deep!" said Thudd. "Could bury tallest mountain there!"

"Why is it so deep?" asked Andrew.

meep . . . "Crust of earth always movin',"

said Thudd. "New crust get made. Old crust go away. This is place where old crust get dragged inside earth. Crust melt. Get recycled."

Uncle Al nodded. "A dozen astronauts have walked on the moon, but only two people have ever gotten to the bottom of the Challenger Deep. The moon is a safer place!"

"Then we'd better get the Water Bug moving again," said Judy, "before we fall into this stupid pit."

"Could the Water Bug be out of fuel?" asked Andrew.

Uncle Al shook his head. "The Water Bug runs on water," he said.

Just then, the living lights of the ocean disappeared. The Water Bug was surrounded by a thick, swirling blackness!

"Woofers!" said Andrew. "We're in some weird smoke cloud!"

"What did you say?" asked Uncle Al. His eyebrows rose in alarm.

Judy and Andrew looked down through the glass floor of the Water Bug. Tall, craggy towers on the ocean floor were spitting out billows of smoke.

"It looks like a witch's castle," Judy said, "with smoking chimneys! How could there be a fire in the *ocean*?"

"Smokey the Bear on a chocolate chip

cookie!" said Uncle Al. "Watch out! You guys are sinking into a—"

Without warning, the Uncle Al hologram popped like a bubble and disappeared.

meep . . . "Black smoker!" said Thudd.

"Black smoker?" said Judy. "What kind of weird-o thing is *that*?"

meep . . . "Ocean floor got deep cracks. Hot, hot, hot down there! Two thousand degrees! Water down there get hot, too. Boil up through cracks. Water drag up lotsa black stuff from crust of earth. Look like smoke. Black stuff pile up in big heaps. Make strange chimneys."

Judy groaned. "So we've got a Water Bug that's getting squashed, we've got no power, and we're falling into boiling water!"

meep . . . "Boiling water not as hot as water here," said Thudd.

"Oh, that's just *great*!" said Judy.

The Water Bug kept sinking through

the bubbling smoke. As Andrew squinted through the windshield, he noticed that the glass looked a little . . . wavy.

"Thudd, what's happening to the windshield?" asked Andrew.

meep . . . "Don't want to say," said Thudd.

"Why not?" asked Andrew.

meep . . . "Don't want to scare Drewd and Oody," said Thudd.

Andrew shook his head. "I get more scared when I don't know what I'm supposed to be scared about," he said.

meep . . . "Okey-dokey," said Thudd. "Windshield melting."

GETTING CRABBY

"Cheese Louise!" yelled Judy. "If the windows melt, we're history!"

CLUUUNK!

The Water Bug smashed into one of the chimneys. The rubber-blubber buggy bumper bounced them away from the dark, twisted shape and the super-hot water.

The Water Bug sank to the ocean floor. The chimneys towered above them.

"It's like we're in a forest of giant, smoking tree trunks," said Judy. She leaned toward the windshield. "Oh my gosh! There are *flowers* growing on the black smokers!"

Judy was looking at a patch of thick stems much taller than the Water Bug. At the top of each stem, a red blossom shape waved in the water.

meep . . . "Not flowers," said Thudd. "Worms!"

"Worms?" said Judy.

meep . . . "Tube worms," said Thudd. "Worm live inside white tube. Only place on earth this kinda tube worm live is on black smoker chimney."

Little white crabs crept around the tube worms. Thudd hopped onto the dashboard and pointed to a flat rock. Heaped on top was something that looked like a huge pile of tangled pasta.

meep . . . "Spaghetti worms," said Thudd.

"Spaghetti!" said Andrew. "I'm getting hungry."

Judy rolled her eyes. "Disgusting boy," she said.

"Well," said Andrew, "we can't get the Water Bug going. There are pizzas in the refrigerator. We can have a snack and wait for Uncle Al to find us."

Judy frowned. "I sure hope that nasty old Soggy Bob doesn't find us first," she said.

Awk! "Soggy Bob used to be a *good* guy before," said Burpp.

"Before what?" asked Judy.

Awk! "Before he met Doctor Kron-Tox," said Burpp.

"Who's Doctor Kron-Tox?" asked Andrew.

Awk! "Soggy Bob used to walk in his sleep," said Burpp. "One day, he almost fell off a cliff! He went to see a strange scientist named Doctor Kron-Tox to find a cure. Doctor Kron-Tox made Burpp stay outside his laboratory. All Burpp could see was lots of flashing lights.

"When Soggy Bob came out, he was different. Before, he was kind to everyone. He

34

picked up stray cats and let them sleep in his bed."

Judy shook her head. "Flashing lights, huh?" She thought for a minute. "I'll bet Doctor Kron-Tox hypnotized Soggy Bob. I've read you can do that with flashing lights."

"Uh-oh," said Andrew.

"'Uh-oh'?" said Judy. "Those are my least favorite syllables in the whole world!"

"Um, there's something weird over there," said Andrew.

"Where?" asked Judy.

"It's crawling from behind the black smoker," said Andrew.

Then Judy saw what Andrew saw.

It was a monster crab! Its body looked like a barrel. Its long, skinny legs spread as wide as the Water Bug.

Behind that crab was another . . . and another. It was a monster-crab army!

meep . . . "Giant spider crab!" said Thudd.

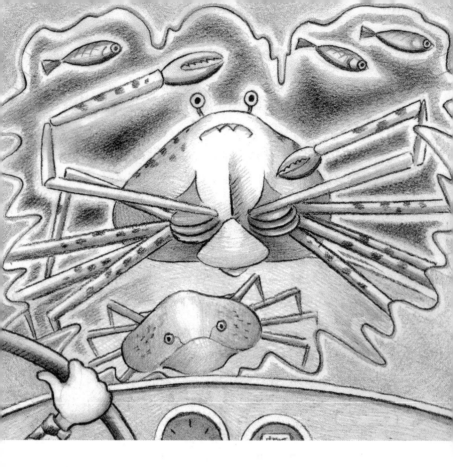

"Biggest crab! Japanese name is *shinin gani*—mean 'dead man's crab.' Giant spider crab eat people that drown!"

"Eeew!" said Judy.

Suddenly gloppy brown goo splattered against the Water Bug's windshield.

The crabs charged toward the Water Bug!

"Andrew! *Do* something!" yelled Judy.

Andrew cranked the key in the ignition and slammed the gas pedal. But the Water Bug still wouldn't start.

The crabs crawled onto the hood. They looked through the windshield with round black eyes on stalks. They snapped at the doors with their claws.

Judy shuddered and shrank into her seat.

kk . . . kkk . . . kkkkk crackled the speaker on the dashboard.

"Oh no!" Andrew hollered. "It's Soggy Bob!"

6 GETTING CRABBIER

"Well, howdy-do!" came the growly voice of Soggy Bob. Andrew looked around but couldn't see Soggy Bob's vehicle.

"It's mah lucky day!" Soggy Bob continued. "Ah finally found ya little mud puppies! Ah see ya met mah little crab friends. They *love* that rotten tuna fish juice ah sprayed onto yer silly vehicle! Heh, heh, heh!"

meep . . . "Crab like rotty food!" said Thudd.

Suddenly the Water Bug began to move. The crabs were pushing it!

Andrew pressed the black Octo-Tool button on the dashboard and yelled into the microphone, "Stop the crabs!"

The hood popped open. The Octo-Tool tentacles slithered out, wrapped themselves around a crab, and flung it away. But the other crabs were nipping the tips of the Octo-Tool tentacles!

"Octo-Tool!" yelled Andrew. "Get back in here!"

But the Octo-Tool kept fighting bravely.

"Get those tentacles back in here *now*!" yelled Andrew.

The Octo-Tool finally untangled its tentacles from the crab claws, curled up under the hood, and slammed it shut.

The crabs began pushing and shoving the Water Bug. It was like they were playing a game of ocean hockey!

Andrew lurched into Judy. *Klink! Klink! Klink!* came the sound of Burpp bouncing around in the back.

"Whoa!" said Soggy Bob. "Ah hear some-thin' over there! Ah know that sound! It's mah parrot shakin' his tail feathers! Ya kids kidnapped mah bird!"

Usually, Soggy Bob couldn't hear any sounds from the Water Bug. But now he could. That's because Burpp was wearing a pair of headphones and a microphone.

Awk! "No!" said Burpp. "The Dubble kids didn't kidnap Burpp. They rescued Burpp!"

"Ya better get yer fool feathers over here right now!" said Soggy Bob. "Ya belong to *me*!"

Awk! "No!" said Burpp. "Burpp is staying here. Burpp won't help you turn giant squids into giant squidwiches!"

Burpp turned off his speaker headphones and tossed them into Judy's lap.

Just then, the Water Bug began to tip. It tumbled over! Andrew's head bumped against the ceiling. The crabs were rolling the Water Bug along the ocean floor!

"Super nutso!" yelled Judy. "What are these stupid crabs going to do with us?"

"I don't know," said Andrew, "but at least they're not trying to eat us."

"*Yet!*" said Judy.

By the Water Bug's headlights, they could see tall shadows looming ahead—underwater hills and mountains.

In front of them was a narrow space between two rocky hills.

Screeeeeek!

The Water Bug scratched against the rocks. The crabs were pushing them through!

Beyond was nothing but the blackest blackness.

It's as dark as the inside of a dog's nose, thought Andrew.

"Where are we?" asked Judy.

Thudd pressed one of the buttons in the middle of his chest. The button popped open and a bright blue beam zoomed out. Thudd pointed the beam down into the dark below them.

meep . . . "Seven miles deep!" said Thudd. "Challenger Deep!"

"Holy moly!" said Andrew.

The Water Bug teetered on the edge. It wobbled. It tumbled over!

"Heh! Heh! Heh!" Soggy Bob's hoarse laugh filled the Water Bug. "So long, little guppies. Sleep tight. Don't let the fangtooth bite! Heh! Heh! Heh!"

7

A BIG ORANGE HEAD!

The Water Bug spun down into the blackness.

"Yikes!" yelled Judy.

"Eek!" squeaked Thudd.

Awk! squawked Burpp.

"Yergh!" yelled Andrew.

KLANK! KLANK! came the sound of the Water Bug banging against the rocky canyon wall.

This is like when you're falling in a dream, thought Andrew. *It feels like you're never going to stop.*

"Cheese Louise!" hollered Judy. "There's a *head* out there!"

A silly-looking orange head about the size of a basketball floated in front of the windshield. It had a frilly collar and flapping elephant ears.

meep . . . "Dumbo octopus!" said Thudd.

"You mean like Dumbo the elephant?" said Andrew. "With big ears that made it fly?"

"Yoop!" said Thudd. "But Dumbo octopus not got ears. Dumbo octopus got fins!"

"He has such beautiful blue eyes!" said Judy.

A creature that looked like a chubby bath toy passed by Andrew's window.

The Dumbo octopus flapped toward it. The bath toy began to glow bright red! Suddenly its glowing skin peeled away, and the squishy little creature threw it at the octopus!

meep . . . "Octopus chase sea cucumber animal," said Thudd. "Sea cucumber make skin light up. Throw skin onto octopus. Bright red skin like big sign! Say 'Eat Me!' to predator animals."

GRAAACK!

Andrew and Judy turned to see that the crack in the back window now zigzagged all the way to the bottom!

"The Water Bug is shrinking again!" yelled Judy. "We're going to get squashed by a zillion tons of ocean!"

"Uncle Al is on his way," said Andrew. "He'll probably find us before we get squashed."

Judy folded her arms across her chest. "We can't count on that," she said. "We need to fix the Water Bug *now*. Let's think about the problem.

"We know the Water Bug stopped working when Burpp arrived. Maybe something got broken accidentally when we dragged Burpp in."

Andrew scratched his head and looked at Burpp. "Maybe you caught a claw on a tube or something," he said.

Awk! "Maybe," said Burpp, shrugging his

wings. "Burpp broke a claw under there."

"I'll look under the hood," said Andrew. "Maybe I can see what's wrong."

Andrew pulled up the flap under the steering wheel.

Plurp! Plurp! Plurp!

There was a drip! But where was it coming from?

It was too dark to see.

Andrew reached into one of his front pockets, pulled out his mini-flashlight, and turned it on.

Then he saw it. A blue tube was dripping big drops. It was the water tube to the fuel system, and it was broken!

"Burpp!" yelled Andrew. "Could you find some tape? Look under the sink."

Awk! "Okay," said Burpp.

Thunk!

He pulled open the cabinet under the sink with his beak.

Awk! "I see soap and paper plates. There's a salami and a bag of marshmallows. But I don't see tape."

"Check the toolbox," said Andrew.

Awk! "No tape there," said Burpp.

I need something to fix this leak, thought Andrew. *Or we could be stuck in an awfully deep place for, um, a long time.*

Andrew pulled his head out from under the hood and looked around.

The Dumbo octopus was outside Andrew's window. The glowing sea cucumber skin was stuck to its head.

Andrew pressed the Octo-Tool button.

"Get the sea cucumber skin from the octopus," he said, "and bring it inside."

The Octo-Tool crept out from under the hood and snuck up behind the octopus. The tentacles snatched the glowing skin, hurried back under the hood, and poked the skin through the flap under the steering wheel.

Andrew grabbed the sea cucumber skin and ducked back under the hood.

He wrapped the skin tightly around the leak and tied a knot.

"Wowzers schnauzers!" said Andrew. "I think this will work!"

When Andrew pulled himself back into the driver's seat, they were settling gently on the bottom of the Challenger Deep.

Outside, the water was dark and empty. Even the little octopus had disappeared. The ground was flat and the color of dirty snow.

meep . . . "Thirty-six thousand feet underwater!" said Thudd. "Deepest place on earth!"

8

MY, WHAT BIG TENTACLES YOU HAVE!

"Super-duper pooper-scooper!" Andrew cheered. "Now four people and two robots have been here! We should celebrate!"

"We should *get out of here*!" said Judy. "Before we get crushed by tons of water. Besides, this place is super creepy. There's nothing *alive* down here."

Awk! "Yes, there is!" said Burpp. He pecked at the windshield.

It was hard to see, but lying completely flat on the ground was a flounder. Its two eyes were on one side of its body. The color of its skin matched the color of the sand exactly.

And crawling up to it was a sea cucumber.

"See," said Andrew, "stuff lives even down here."

"Strange-a-mundo!" said Judy. "But if the water presses against them like tons of elephants, how come these guys don't get crushed?"

meep . . . "Cuz fish made of water," said Thudd. "Water not crush water. Water crush space filled with air. Fish down here not got air spaces inside."

IRRRRK! The Water Bug trembled. Then the windshield bulged out!

"The Water Bug is shrinking again!" Judy yelled. "We've got to get out of here *now*!"

"Uh-oh!" said Andrew. He turned the key in the ignition and shoved the gas pedal to the floor. "Let's hope the Water Bug works!"

Brrrrrrr . . . came the sound of the Water Bug's paddle wheels spinning.

Andrew pulled up on the steering wheel.

The Water Bug shot up from the canyon floor.

"Yay!" shouted Andrew.

"Yippee!" squeaked Thudd.

Awk! squawked Burpp.

"Finally!" shouted Judy.

The Water Bug paddled up through the water. Now and then, the headlights fell on a sea star or a herd of sea cucumbers crawling along the canyon walls.

"I see hills up there!" said Judy. "We're almost at the top of the Challenger Deep!"

"I hope we can catch up with Soggy Bob," said Andrew. "He's had a lot of time to get ahead of us."

Suddenly the words GIANT SQUID at the top of the compass began to blink orange. The compass needle twitched nervously.

Andrew's eyes grew wide.

"Wowzers schnauzers!" he said. "I wonder if this means we're getting close to the giant squid."

"Or if the compass is broken," said Judy.

The Water Bug was just below the rocky hills at the edge of the canyon. A stone pillar rose above. Something long and thick and red was twitching around it.

"What's that?" asked Andrew. He steered the Water Bug closer to it.

"Jeepers creepers!" yelled Andrew. "It's a—"

"Giant tentacle!" yelled Judy.

meep . . . "Giant squid!" said Thudd.

As the Water Bug paddled up, its head-lights fell on two black eyes bigger than basketballs!

The squid seemed to be looking at something beyond the Water Bug. Its smooth, rubbery skin changed from red to rose to white.

Clik clik clik . . . Clik clik clik . . . Clik clik clik . . .

Andrew turned toward the sound.

It looked like a humongous lumpy rock was swimming toward the giant squid.

meep . . . "Sperm whale!" said Thudd. "Sperm whale make clicking sounds like dolphin. Sound bounce off of stuff. Find prey animal. Find giant squid!"

The whale sped toward the squid like the engine of a train. The torpedo-shaped squid jetted out from the rocks. It flickered colors like a neon sign.

The whale's head was as wide as the Water Bug. When the whale opened its mouth, its bottom jaw was longer than the Water Bug, but it was thin—only as wide as one of the Water Bug's seats!

Thudd pointed to the sharp yellow hills that lined the whale's bottom jaw.

meep . . . "Sperm whale got biggest teeth

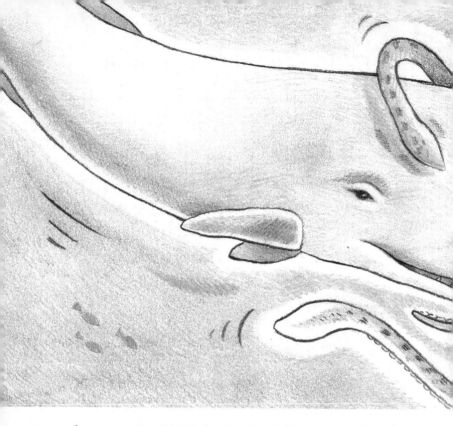

of any animal! Eight inches! Big as teeth of *Tyrannosaurus* dinosaur!" said Thudd.

The whale lunged toward the squid. The giant squid was faster than the whale. It zoomed away.

Then the Water Bug's headlights fell on another monster head—another sperm whale!

It swooped toward the giant squid. The

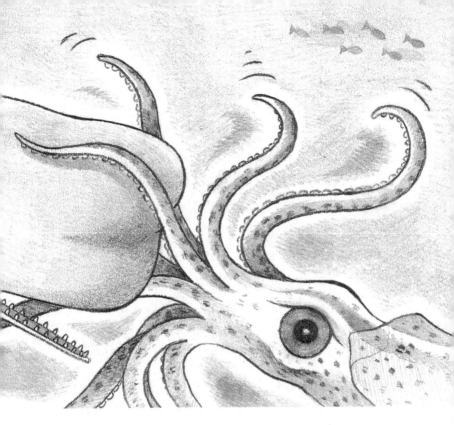

squid's two longest tentacles—as long as
school buses—whizzed past the whale's front
teeth. The whale chomped down, but not fast
enough to catch the squid.

The ends of the squid's longest tentacles
were shaped like clubs. They lashed at the
whale. Where the clubs hit the whale's skin,
they left big, round marks.

meep . . . "Squid got suckers on tentacles," said Thudd. "Suckers got teeth around edges. Grab prey tight."

Just then, the headlights glinted on something silver behind a rocky hill.

kk . . . kkk . . . kkkkk came a familiar sound through the speaker. It was followed by a gruff voice that made Andrew and Judy jump.

"Well, ah'll be a barnacle's brother!" said Soggy Bob. "Ah thought ya water rascals were sunk for good! Well, now ya get to see me make mah biggest catch. Ah can almost taste them squidwiches now! Gotta get me some big buns. Heh! Heh! Heh!"

BAAAAROOOOOOM!

It was a huge underwater explosion!

DEAD OR ALIVE?

The whales sped off into the darkness.

For a moment, the giant squid was as still as a statue. Then it dropped to the ocean floor. Its tentacles looked like a pile of gigantic pasta.

kk . . . kkk . . . kkkkk

"Heh, heh, heh," chuckled Soggy Bob. "Ah guess mah fireworks were a little bit shocking."

"Is it dead?" asked Judy.

meep . . . "Maybe not dead," said Thudd. "Maybe shocked. Hafta wait and see if squid move."

The Crab-Mobile crept from behind the rocky hill. The green glow of its glass dome lit up Soggy Bob's grinning face.

kk . . . kkk . . . kkkkk

"The giant squid is *mine!*" said Soggy Bob.

The round door at the front of the Crab-Mobile slid open and a big net swirled out. The Crab-Mobile's claws grabbed the net by its edges and dragged it toward the giant squid.

"*Noooo!*" yelled Judy. "We can't let Soggy Bob turn the giant squid into snacks! We've worked so hard to save it!"

"But if we get too close," said Andrew, "we'll get caught in the net, too."

Suddenly Thudd's purple button started to blink. Uncle Al appeared at the end of a purple beam.

"Hey, guys!" he said happily. "Look behind you!"

Andrew and Judy turned and saw a vehicle

shaped like a huge sea horse. It was covered with round porthole windows and it glowed with a deep blue light.

Judy smiled and waved with both hands. "It's the See Horse!" she said. "Uncle Al found us!"

The See Horse flashed orange lights from its portholes.

"Look at that!" said Judy. "The See Horse is saying 'Hello' in Morse code!"

"Uh-oh," said Andrew. "Look!" The Crab-Mobile's claws were tucking the net around the squid.

"Wait a minute," said Judy. "Soggy Bob was a good guy before Doctor Kron-Tox hypnotized him with flashing lights. We've got lots of flashing lights here. If we could hypnotize Soggy Bob, maybe he'd go back to his old pussycat-loving self. Then he'd let go of the giant squid!"

Awk! "Smart little Dubble!" said Burpp.

He poked his beak into Judy's frizzy hair and untangled a knot.

"Let's start blinking!" said Andrew. "Uncle Al, you blink, too!"

Andrew jiggled the switch that turned the Water Bug's headlights on and off.

Uncle Al flashed lime-green lights from the windows of the See Horse.

Soggy Bob pushed his face close to the

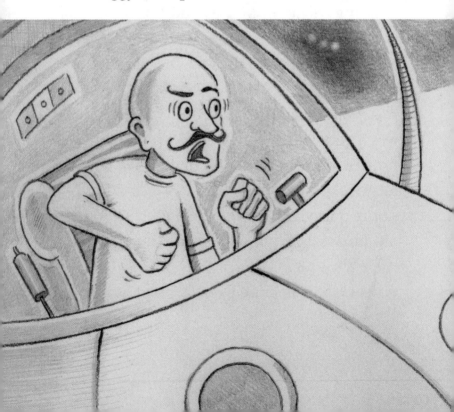

glass dome of the Crab-Mobile. His eyes opened wide. He looked surprised. Then he shook his fists.

But after a minute, he slouched in his seat. His head slumped toward the windshield.

meep . . . "Soggy Bob in a trance," said Thudd. "Not awake, not asleep. Now is time

to give good message to Soggy Bob. Change bad message from Doctor Kron-Tox."

Judy grabbed Burpp's speaker head-phones.

"Can you hear me, Mr. Soggy Bob?" she asked.

"Yeah," said Soggy Bob quietly. "But ah'm feelin' kinda sleepy right now." His head tipped forward. "Ah want mah bunny slip-pers," he sighed.

Andrew grabbed Burpp's headphones.

"Mr. Soggy Bob," said Andrew, "you want to go back to the good person you used to be. The person who loves animals and takes care of them."

Soggy Bob nodded his sagging head.

"Ah sure do," said Soggy Bob. "And ah want mah friend Burpp back. Ah miss the lit-tle guy."

Burpp pushed himself between the front seats.

His beak poked into Andrew's shoulder. Andrew saw something wet dripping from Burpp's eyes.

Could those be tears? Andrew wondered. *Can robots cry?*

Urf, urf, urf! came a sound through the speaker.

Soggy Bob was crying, too!

"Wake up, Mr. Soggy Bob! Everything's okay!" said Andrew.

Soggy Bob lifted his head and looked around.

"Where am ah?" he asked. "What am ah doin' here? And what's *that*?"

Soggy Bob was staring at the giant squid wrapped in the net.

"Oh mah gosh!" he said. "It's a poor little giant squid! And it's all tangled up! Ah've got to get it out of there. Hey! You over there in those strange-lookin' vehicles! Can ya give me a hand?"

"Sure we can!" said Andrew.

"Here we come!" said Uncle Al.

Andrew zoomed the Water Bug close to the giant squid.

Under the net, it looked like a big balloon in a Thanksgiving Day parade—before it was blown up.

"I hope it's still alive," said Andrew.

Judy shook her head. "It doesn't look good."

ALOHA!

Andrew pressed a black button on the dash-board. "Remove net from giant squid," he said.

Uncle Al used the wiggly tail of the See Horse to help. The Crab-Mobile's claws tugged the net all the way off and dragged it through its round door.

"Its eyes are so amazing!" said Judy, look-ing into the black platter-sized disks.

meep . . . "Biggest eyes of any animal!" said Thudd. "Maybe use eyes to find animals with living light. Then eat 'em!"

The See Horse shined a spotlight on the

tentacles that drooped around the squid's mouth. There were ten of them. Two of them were much longer and thinner than the others. The eight shorter ones were as thick as fire hoses.

Uncle Al shined the light on the eight shorter tentacles.

"These are the squid's feeding tentacles," said Uncle Al. "The squid uses them to stuff food into its mouth."

Uncle Al traced the two longest tentacles with the spotlight. "The squid uses these to hunt," he said.

"I can see the suckers!" Andrew said.

Each of the feeding tentacles had two rows of circle-shaped suckers. The suckers were the size of silver dollars. Around each sucker was a ring of small, sharp teeth!

meep . . . "Squid hang on to prey with suckers," said Thudd. "Squid fight sperm whale with suckers, too."

Inside the circle of tentacles was the giant squid's mouth—a beak as big as a man's hand.

Awk! "It's got a beak like me!" squawked Burpp.

meep . . . "Squid beak strong, strong, strong!" said Thudd. "Bite through steel!"

"Wait a minute," said Uncle Al. "This guy looks even bigger than a regular giant squid. I want to get a closer look at these hunting tentacles."

The club-like shapes at the ends of the long tentacles had suckers with swiveling hooks.

"Good golly, Miss Molly!" yelled Uncle Al. "This isn't a giant squid! An ordinary giant squid doesn't have hooks on its suckers. The animal that does is . . . the *colossal* squid!"

Suddenly one of the squid's hunting tentacles began to twitch.

"Jumping gerbils!" said Andrew. "The squid's *alive!*"

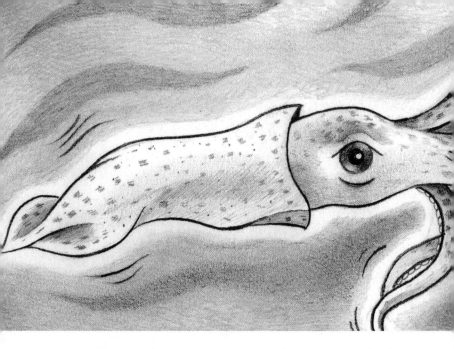

The other hunting tentacle snaked through the water. The tentacles around the squid's mouth began to wiggle. The colossal squid sprang to life!

Its tentacles shot toward the Crab-Mobile and wrapped around it.

meep . . . "Squid love to eat crab!" said Thudd.

"Hey there, big squid fella!" said Soggy Bob. He was shaking. "Hold yer horses! Ah don't mean ya no harm!"

Awk! "Got to save Soggy Bob!" said Burpp.

"But how can we get near the squid?" asked Andrew.

Uncle Al spoke up. "I'll try to communicate with it."

Uncle Al drove the See Horse between the squid and the Crab-Mobile. The See Horse flickered red, then purple, then pink.

The colossal squid turned a deep red. It removed a tentacle from the Crab-Mobile and lashed out at the See Horse!

The See Horse dashed away from the squid.

Uncle Al shook his head. "I think the See Horse looks too different. The colossal squid may think it's an enemy—or something to eat."

"You know," said Judy, "the Water Bug with the Octo-Tool looks kind of like a squid. Maybe *it* can communicate with the colossal squid."

"Too risky," said Uncle Al.

"We've got to try," said Judy.

Andrew pressed the black Octo-Tool button and spoke into the microphone. "Tell the colossal squid we're all friends," he said. "Tell it that we'll never bother it again."

The Octo-Tool crept out bravely. It twirled its tentacles to get the squid's attention.

The Water Bug glowed bright blue, then purple, then red—the same red as the colossal squid.

The squid let go of the Crab-Mobile— then it jetted toward the Water Bug. Its tentacles waved like the tails of angry cats.

"Let's all get out of here *now*!" said Andrew.

He pushed the Octo-Tool button.

"Start escape jet!" he yelled. A fat black tube popped out from under the hood.

"Follow me, guys!" said Uncle Al. "We're going back to Hawai'i!"

The Water Bug, the Crab-Mobile, and the See Horse raced through the twinkling ocean. It seemed as vast as the sky!

It was only when the sea began to turn from black to blue that Andrew and Judy realized how tired they were.

As the underwater vehicles rose, the sun's rays made a sparkling ceiling above them. Andrew and Judy had been awake for nearly twenty-four hours! Andrew was almost too sleepy to drive.

Suddenly Judy yelled, "It's him!"

"Huh?" mumbled Andrew, snapping awake. "What? Who?"

"It's Nahu!" said Judy, tapping on her window.

A dolphin was tapping his beak outside Judy's window. The dolphin had a big bite mark in his tail. It was the same dolphin they'd met when they started their under-water adventure!

"So, guys," said Uncle Al through his hologram, "we'll be in Hawai'i in a few minutes. I've got some strange things to tell you. Who wants to have some breakfast pizza?"

"Wowzers schnauzers!" said Andrew. "I want sausage and mushrooms!"

"Breakfast sounds great," said Judy. "As long as I don't have to hear about any weird stuff."

meep . . . "Comin', Unkie!" said Thudd.

Awk! "Burpp would love to come. But Soggy Bob and Burpp have got to get back to our kitties. Burpp will miss you, little Dub-bles," Burpp said.

In the rearview mirror, Andrew could see that Burpp's eyes were wet again.

Uncle Al looked disappointed. "Sorry that Burpp and Soggy Bob can't join us," he said. "Because the story I have to tell is stranger than a giant squid. And it's about Doctor Kron-Tox. He's not just hypnotizing people anymore—he's hiding them."

"Where's he hiding them?" asked Andrew.

"Now, that's the strange part," said Uncle Al. "I think he's hiding them—in time!"

TO BE CONTINUED IN ANDREW, JUDY, AND THUDD'S
NEXT EXCITING ADVENTURE:

ANDREW LOST
IN TIME!

In stores November 2004

TRUE STUFF

THUDD

Thudd wanted to tell you more about the strange things that happen in the deep, but he was too busy helping Andrew and Judy save the giant squid. Here's what Thudd wanted to say:

• The "living light" of most creatures comes from bacteria that live in the animals' cells. These cells are often like little eyes that can open and close. The relationship between bacteria and bioluminescent animals is an example of symbiosis—creatures living together. In this kind of symbiosis, called mutualism, both creatures benefit from the relationship. The bacteria get food and protection from the animal. The animal gets the ability to produce light.

• "SOS" stands for "Save our ship." This is the signal that sailors flash from sinking boats. SOS became the short way to say "Help!" in Morse code.

• It's very hot inside the earth. That's why there are volcanoes and black smoker chimneys. This heat is left over from when the earth was formed more than 4 billion years ago!

• Baby earth began with huge rocks smashing together in space. Smashing creates heat. This heat got trapped inside the earth. (For a small demonstration, try clapping your hands together a lot. Your hands will get very warm!)

• Almost all life on earth and in the sea is fueled by the energy of the sun. All plants need sunlight to grow. Plants are eaten by plant-eaters. Plant-eaters are eaten by meat-eaters. So without sunlight, plant-eaters and meat-eaters would have no food. But near the black smokers, many creatures live on molecules that boil up from inside the earth. These are the only places on earth where life does not depend on the sun.

• Some sea stars (we used to call them starfish, but they're not fish!) eat by throwing their stomachs outside their bodies to digest their prey! When the animal is completely digested, the stomach is pulled back into the sea star's body.

• What's the biggest animal on earth? If we go by weight, it's the blue whale. If we judge by length, it's the lion's mane jellyfish. These can be as big as washing machines, with 200-foot-long tentacles!

• Sea cucumbers eat dirt! They suck sand off the ocean floor, digest the bacteria and little pieces of dead stuff, and poop out the sand! Some sea cucumbers can throw their guts at predators! This scares the predator and gives it a nice snack. In a few weeks, the sea cucumber will grow a new set of intestines!

• How do sperm whales hunt giant squids in the black waters of the deep? No one knows for sure. One idea is that sperm whales make sounds that shock the squids and make them easier to catch.

Find out more weird stuff!

Visit www.AndrewLost.com.

THUDD

WHERE TO FIND MORE TRUE STUFF

Want to find out about the amazing and mysterious things that can happen in the underwater world? Check these out!

• *Dolphin Adventure* by Wayne Grover (New York: Avon, 2000). This is the true story of how a family of dolphins asked humans for help to save their injured baby!

• *Shark Lady: True Adventures of Eugenie Clark* by Ann McGovern (New York: Scholastic, 1987) and *Adventures of the Shark Lady: Eugenie Clark Around the World* by Ann McGovern (New York: Scholastic, 1998). In these books, a nine-year-old girl who loves to watch the fish in her aquarium grows up to study sea creatures all over the world. She swims with flashlight fish, rides a monster whale shark, and gets caught in the claws of a giant spider crab!

• *Eyewitness: Ocean* by Miranda Macquitty (New York: DK Publishing, 2000). Lots of information and great pictures tell the story of the oceans—how they were made, what lives in them, and how we explore them.

• *Oceans* by Seymour Simon (New York: HarperCollins Children's Books, 1997). You'll feel the waves when you see these pictures! Lots of great information, too. For example, there are 100 billion gallons of water in the ocean for each person on earth!

• *Sea Jellies: Rainbows in the Sea* by Elizabeth Tayntor Gowell (London: Franklin Watts, 1993). Jellyfish aren't fish. They don't have hearts or brains or bones, but they hunt and eat and reproduce. They can be smaller than your fingernail or bigger than a washing machine. You can find out how these blobby creatures live and see lots of them in this book.

• *Tentacles: Tales of the Giant Squid* by Shirley Raye Redmond (New York: Random House, 2003). Hungry to know more about these mysterious creatures? Munch on this book, as well as . . .

• *Giant Squid: Mystery of the Deep* by Jennifer Dussling (New York: Grosset & Dunlap, 1999).

• *Sea Monsters: Search for the Giant Squid* (National Geographic Video, 1998). You won't see *giant* squids, but you'll see some awfully big ones! Watch their amazing color changes as they come after a man who is trying to study them!

Turn the page
for a sneak peek at
Andrew, Judy, and Thudd's
next exciting adventure—

ANDREW LOST
IN TIME!

Available November 2004

TICK . . . TOCK . . . TICK . . . TOCK . . .

"No onions on my pizza, please," said Andrew Dubble. "They remind me of when we were attacked by deadly snails on the coral reef!"

Uncle Al's face crinkled into a smile. "The onions protected you from the snails," he said. "They saved your life!"

Andrew and his thirteen-year-old cousin Judy were sitting in the big, comfortable kitchen of Uncle Al's log cabin in Montana. Just a few hours ago, they had been deep in the Pacific Ocean rescuing a giant squid.

Uncle Al loaded a thick, cheesy slice of pizza onto a plate.

Judy pulled at a string of hot cheese that had gotten tangled in her long, frizzy hair.

"It's too bad we had to leave Hawai'i so fast this morning," she said. "We didn't even have time to eat breakfast or say good-bye to our friends."

meep . . . "Uncle Al had to come back," came a squeaky voice from Andrew's shirt pocket. "Big trouble!"

It was Andrew's best friend, Thudd, a little silver robot invented by Uncle Al. "Thudd" was short for The Handy Ultra-Digital Detective.

Uncle Al nodded. His smile dimmed.

"Sorry for the big rush," he said. "My assistant, Winka Wilde, is missing. There was a strange message on my Hologram Helper. I'll let you hear it."

Uncle Al pulled a round purple object the size of a golf ball from his pocket. He pressed a black button at the top of it.

Tick . . . tock . . . tick . . . tock . . . came a

soft sound. Then a deep voice began to speak slowly:

Time is short,
Time is long.
Time is a chain.
Its links are strong.

But I've found the way
To break time's hold.
I tuck who I want
Into time's many folds.

Miss Wilde is gone.
I'm sure you're vexed.
But don't worry, Dubble.
You'll be next!

Don't look to the future,
Don't study the present.
She's locked in the past—
And it's *sooo* unpleasant!

"HA! HA! HA!" came echo-y laughter.

Tick . . . tock . . . tick . . . tock . . .

The message ended.

Judy shivered. "That voice gives me the creeps," she said.

"I know that you guys have heard about Doctor Kron-Tox," said Uncle Al.

"Yeah," said Andrew. "He hypnotized Soggy Bob to get him to hunt for the giant squid."

Uncle Al nodded and poured some grape juice for Judy and Andrew.

"That was the voice of Doctor Kron-Tox," said Uncle Al. "I used to work with him. He was the smartest man I ever knew. His ideas were amazing.

"But he became greedy. He started taking credit for other people's inventions. He tried to control people.

"Then he became obsessed with time. That's all he could think about. He left our laboratory and no one knows where he went. But we do know that two important inventors are missing. Winka Wilde is one of them. And when these inventors disappeared, we got that message from Doctor Kron-Tox."

meep . . . "Unkie Al gotta be careful," said Thudd.

"Don't worry," said Uncle Al. "The worst enemy of a bad problem is a good plan.

"Five months ago, I started working on an invention that may be able to travel through time. It's called the Time-A-Tron. It's not finished yet. But in a few days, it will be ready to test."

"Wowzers schnauzers!" said Andrew. "Where is it?"

"Are you kidding?" said Judy. "Nobody can travel through time."

meep . . . "Want to see!" said Thudd.

"Well, let's go!" said Uncle Al, pulling open the heavy wooden door that led outside. It was beginning to get dark.

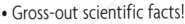

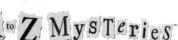